Gentle Giant

by Michael Morpurgo

illustrated by Michael Foreman

On a small island way out in the middle of a silver lake there once lived a sad young man. He had been unhappy ever since he was a child, when his mother had died and left him alone in the world, still quite unable to talk.

But he was sad for another reason too. He had grown up into a giant of a man, very big, very strong and very frightening. Because of this, no-one liked to go near him, and so he had no friends at all.

Every day he rowed across the silver lake to work in the village of Ballyloch, where he thatched all the houses and barns and hayricks with barley straw. But, however hard he worked, the villagers were always unkind. If ever he opened his mouth to try to talk they simply laughed at him. "He caws like a crow," they jeered. "He croaks like a frog."

They called him the Beastman of Ballyloch.

"The Beastman's coming," the villagers would cry. "Look out, look out, Mister Ugly's about!" Time and again they warned their children to keep away from him. "He's mad. He's bad," they said. "He'll gobble you up for his supper. Don't go near him."

Every evening after work, the Beastman would row back to his island home where he lived on his own. But he was never quite alone, for around him lived all the wild creatures he loved – squirrels, otters, ducks, herons, kingfishers – and dearest of all, his beloved swans. To every one of them he was neither a Beastman nor ugly, but a true and trusted friend.

Early one spring morning the Beastman looked out over the lake and saw there was already someone out fishing. It was a young woman in a wide-brimmed straw hat. And then she began to sing. The Beastman had never heard anything so beautiful.

But suddenly, as he watched, the boat tipped, and with a cry the girl was over the side, vanishing at once under the water. The Beastman did not think twice. He ran down to the lake and plunged in. He swam out to where her straw hat still floated, and dived down into the murky depths beneath. It was icy cold in the water, but the Beastman searched and searched until at last he found her, lying in amongst the weeds at the bottom of the lake.

Gathering her in his arms he swam up to the surface and back to his island. He did all he could to bring her back to life, but still she did not move and she did not breathe. The Beastman held his face in his hands and wept.

"Why are you crying?" She was speaking! She was alive after all! "You saved me," she said.

He wanted so much to talk, to tell her how happy he was, but all that came out was a hideous croaking.

She smiled at him. "Back home in the village, we call you the Beastman of Ballyloch. But you're not a Beastman, are you? All I see in your eyes is gentleness."

She took his hand. "My name is Miranda," she told him, "and I shall be your friend for ever."

All that day Miranda rested by the fire, while the Beastman made the best potato soup she had ever tasted. As she slept, he looked down at her and knew that he loved her more than life itself.

That evening, as they rowed back over the silver lake, she could see that he was sad. "I'll come back again tomorrow," she promised. "Don't worry."

But someone had seen them out together in the Beastman's boat. By the time she got home, her father knew all about it, and he was furious. "You dare to disobey me! Haven't I told you never, ever, to go near that monster?"

Miranda tried to explain how the Beastman had saved her life, but her father was too angry to listen. He took her upstairs and locked her in her room.

That same evening, there came to the village a stranger, a smiling stranger with twinkling eyes. He was carrying a load of sacks on the back of his cart.

"What do you want most in all the world?" he asked the villagers.

"To be rich, of course," they cried.

"And so you shall be, my friends, but only if you buy my magic stardust. All you have to do is sprinkle my magic stardust on your lake. Believe me, within one day you will be catching fish as big as whales."

And they believed every word he told them. With his twinkling eyes he charmed them, and in no time at all the villagers had bought all the stardust he had.

Next morning, early, they were out in their fishing boats sprinkling the stardust on the water. By evening the silver lake rang with shouts of joy. The stardust was doing its magic! They were catching the biggest, fattest fish they had ever seen.

But the Beastman was becoming more and more troubled. His swans and all his wild creatures seemed suddenly bewildered and frightened, as if they knew that something terrible was about to happen. And still Miranda had not come back to him as she had promised.

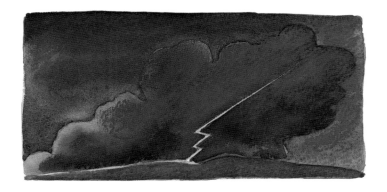

That night, thunder rumbled and rolled about the mountains. Lightning crackled, and the lake howled all around him in the wind. The Beastman stood on the shore of his island, waiting and watching for Miranda. But she did not come and she did not come.

By morning, the storm had passed. The Beastman was still standing there, still hoping to see Miranda's boat. But there was no boat. Instead, in the first light of dawn, he saw to his horror that his beautiful lake was no longer silver, but a ghastly green all over.

Then, from across the lake he heard the sound of wailing. He soon saw why. Ballyloch was in ruins. Every roof of every house and barn had been blown off by the storm, and the straw was strewn about the streets. The Beastman crouched down and ran his hand through the water. Slime, green slime.

An otter ran along the shore, green from head to tail. Everywhere the fish lay dead or dying. Worst of all, his beloved swans were choking as they dipped their necks into the water to drink.

That was when the Beastman noticed a bright circle of clear silver water, and floating in the middle of it, was Miranda's straw hat. He waded out and plucked it from the water. Then he saw that underneath, it was covered in thick green slime.

At once, the Beastman knew what had to be done. But he needed help. Miranda. Miranda would help him.

He leapt into his boat and rowed over to Ballyloch. As he hurried through the village streets, no one noticed him. "Our lake is dying," wailed the villagers. "It's the smiling stranger's fault! Where is he?" But the smiling stranger had long since taken his money and vanished.

From her bedroom window, Miranda saw the Beastman and called down to him. In no time, he had unlocked her door and set her free.

"Look at the lake!" she cried. "What are we to do?"

At first, Miranda could make no sense of the Beastman's frantic croaking. Only when he held out her straw hat, and showed her the green slime underneath, did she understand what he was trying to tell her.

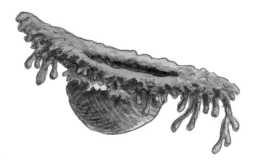

At once, Miranda gathered the villagers together.

"Do you want to save our beautiful silver lake?" she asked them. "And all our wild creatures?"

"Yes!" they cried. So Miranda told them exactly what the Beastman wanted them to do. No one argued, for they knew this was their only hope.

Soon, everyone was busy picking up the fallen thatch from the streets. All day they worked, spreading it out, weaving it into great straw mats. Their backs ached, their hands were raw; but on they worked until at last the job was done. Then, at dusk, the fishing boats towed the mats out on to the lake and left them floating there. "Now all we can do is wait and hope." said Miranda.

That night, out on the island, Miranda and the Beastman gathered together his beloved swans and all the wild creatures they could find, and cleaned them until their feathers and their fur were bright and shining again.

When they had finished, Miranda taught the Beastman to say her name. Soon, he could say 'Manda', which sounded, she told him, just as good as Miranda, if not better. She taught him many more words that night, but his favourite was 'Manda'. He kept saying it over and over, until they both fell asleep.

Next morning they woke to the sound of whooping and cheering and laughing. They could hardly believe their eyes...

Every fishing boat in Ballyloch was out on the lake, and heading towards the island. And the lake was silver again, dancing in the light of the early morning sun. The green had entirely vanished.

And the straw had done its work, just as they had hoped it would.
Overhead flew the Beastman's beloved swans, white again, as
white as snow, their wings singing in the air.

The people of Ballyloch were overjoyed. As for Miranda's father, he begged his daughter's forgiveness, and the Beastman's too, for the way he had been treated for so many years.

"We know now," he said, "how wise you are and kind, for you knew the secret of the barley straw and saved us from ourselves. For as long as men tell stories, they will tell of you – and of Miranda's marvellous hat!"

Everyone hung garlands of flowers around the Beastman's neck, and Miranda's too. All day long they danced and sang and feasted.

As the villagers' boats left the island that evening, the sun went down over the silver lake. Miranda's hand stole into his.

"You are no longer the Beastman of Ballyloch," she whispered. "You are my Gentle Giant."

"And you are my Manda," said the Gentle Giant. "My Manda."

And it's quite true about straw and water.
Lay a mat of straw on a murky green pond for a while,
and the water will soon be bright and clean again.
Try it! There's truth in every fairy tale.

For Jane, her book, M. M.

First published in hardback in Great Britain by HarperCollins Publishers Ltd in 2003
First published in paperback by HarperCollins Children's Books in 2004

3 5 7 9 10 8 6 4 2

ISBN: 0-00-711192-4

HarperCollins Children's Books is a division of HarperCollins Publishers Ltd.

Text copyright © Michael Morpurgo 2003
Illustrations copyright © Michael Foreman 2003

The author and illustrator assert the moral right to be identified
as the author and illustrator of the work.
A CIP catalogue record for this title is available from the British Library.

Visit our website at: www.harpercollinschildrensbooks.co.uk

Printed and bound in China